LiLAH TOV
GOOD NIGHT

Ben Gundersheimer (also known as Mister G)

illustrated by **Noar Lee Naggan**

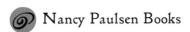 Nancy Paulsen Books

Nancy Paulsen Books

an imprint of Penguin Random House LLC, New York

Visit us online at penguinrandomhouse.com

Library of Congress Cataloging-in-Publication Data
Names: G, Mister, author. | Naggan, Noar Lee, illustrator.
Title: Lilah Tov, good night / Ben Gundersheimer ("Mister G") ; illustrated by Noar Lee Naggan.
Description: New York: Nancy Paulsen Books, [2020] • Summary: "Text based on a Hebrew lullaby tells the story of
a Jewish refugee family traveling by night to find a safe home in a new land"—Provided by publisher.
Identifiers: LCCN 2019008865 | ISBN 9781524740665 (hardcover: alk. paper) | ISBN 9781524740672 (ebook) |
ISBN 9781524740696 (ebook) • Subjects: | CYAC: Bedtime—Fiction. | Jews—Fiction. | Refugees—Fiction.
Classification: LCC PZ8.3.G11 Lil 2020 | DDC [E]—dc23
LC record available at https://lccn.loc.gov/2019008865
Manufactured in China by RR Donnelley Asia Printing Solutions Ltd.
ISBN 9781524740665

Special Markets ISBN: 9780593111871 Not for resale
CIP Code: 042026.6K1/B1491/A2

1 3 5 7 9 10 8 6 4 2
Design by Semadar Megged. Text set in Golden Type ITC Std.
The art was created in pencil and digitally colored in Photoshop.

To the memory of my grandparents,
Herman and Frieda Gundersheimer,
refugees who crossed an ocean for a better life
—B. G.

To my mother, Zmira Lutzky,
the tyger burning bright in the forests of the night
—N. L. N.

It's been a long and
beautiful day

The sun is setting;
light fades away

The moon is rising,
big and bright
Time to wish everyone
good night

Lilah Tov
to the roosters and hens

Lilah Tov
to the bears in their dens

Lilah Tov
to the bats in their caves

Lilah Tov
to the beach and the waves

Lilah Tov
to the clouds in the sky

Lilah Tov
to the stars way up high

Lilah Tov
to the fish in the sea

Lilah Tov
to the birds in the trees

Lilah Tov
to the mountains and streams

Soon you will be
ready for dreams

The house is quiet;
you're tucked in tight

Lilah Tov to you.
Good night.